Dear Parent:
Your child's love of reading starts here!

Every child learns to read in a different way and at his or her own speed. Some go back and forth between reading levels and read favorite books again and again. Others read through each level in order. You can help your young reader improve and become more confident by encouraging his or her own interests and abilities. From books your child reads with you to the first books he or she reads alone, there are I Can Read Books for every stage of reading:

SHARED READING
Basic language, word repetition, and whimsical illustrations, ideal for sharing with your emergent reader

BEGINNING READING
Short sentences, familiar words, and simple concepts for children eager to read on their own

READING WITH HELP
Engaging stories, longer sentences, and language play for developing readers

READING ALONE
Complex plots, challenging vocabulary, and high-interest topics for the independent reader

ADVANCED READING
Short paragraphs, chapters, and exciting themes for the perfect bridge to chapter books

I Can Read Books have introduced children to the joy of reading since 1957. Featuring award-winning authors and illustrators and a fabulous cast of beloved characters, I Can Read Books set the standard for beginning readers.

A lifetime of discovery begins with the magical words "I Can Read!"

Visit www.icanread.com for information
on enriching your child's reading experience.

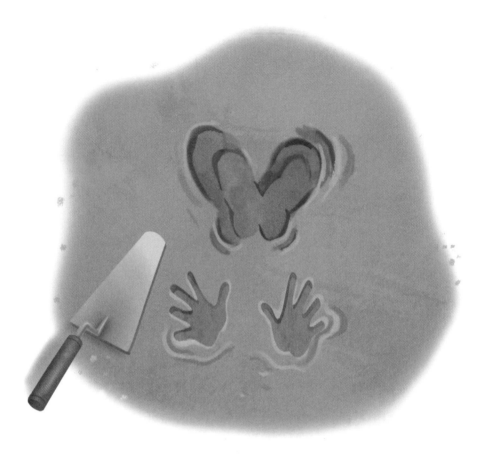

I Can Read Book® is a trademark of HarperCollins Publishers.

Fancy Nancy: Nancy Makes Her Mark
www.icanread.com

ISBN 978-0-06-288865-5 (trade bdg.)—ISBN 978-0-06-279828-2 (pbk.)

Book design by Brenda E. Angelilli and Scott Petrower

18 19 20 21 22   LSCC   10 9 8 7 6 5 4 3 2 1   ❖   First Edition

Nancy Makes Her Mark

Adapted by Nancy Parent
Based on the episode
by Matt Hoverman

Illustrations by the
Disney Storybook
Art Team

HARPER
An Imprint of HarperCollinsPublishers

Ooh la la!

Today, Dad has a big plan.

He wants to surprise Mom and
fix the big crack in the walkway
when she goes out.

I have a big plan too.

I show Bree my pictures.

"Movie stars put handprints in cement for people to come and see," I say. "It makes them memorable!"

That's fancy for famous forever.

I ask Dad if we can put handprints
in the wet cement.

"It will give the walkway pizzazz!" I say.

That's fancy for style.

Dad thinks that's a great plan!

"Mom will love it," he says.

JoJo and Bree

make handprints.

I make handprints too.

"Now we will be famous forever,"

I say.

Dad takes JoJo inside

to clean her up.

I look down at my work.

Hmm, something is missing.

I know what's missing!
The movie stars
didn't just leave handprints.
They left footprints too.

"I'm going to need your help,"

I tell Bree.

Bree helps me balance.

My prints are perfect, at last.

But . . . they're still not very fancy.

"How can we make

our prints fancy?" asks Bree.

"Cement doesn't come with glitter!"

THAT'S IT!

We'll sprinkle glitter on our prints
while the cement is still wet!

"I'll get the glitter!" Bree says.

15

But when Bree goes inside,

my dog Frenchy gets loose.

I run to keep Frenchy away

from the wet cement!

Frenchy chases after a squirrel.

I chase after Frenchy.

But I trip and . . .

SPLAT.

The walkway is ruined!

This is a disaster!

Bree comes back with the glitter.

"Forget about being memorable,"

I tell her.

"The cement is ruined!"

"Dad will be devastated," I say.

That's fancy for disappointed.

Dad and JoJo come back outside.

Dad sees the mess.

He sees me too.

22

"We can fix this

with some new cement," Dad says.

We will have to hurry

before Mom gets back!

We stir the new cement.

Dad spreads it across the walkway.

"Let's make handprints again,"
says Dad.

"Footprints too," he adds.

As I step onto the cement,

I hear a car in the driveway.

Mom is home!

But I'm stuck!

"Grab hold, everyone," says Dad.

Everyone pulls me free!

I look down at the walkway.

"I ruined my footprints!" I say.

Now the cement is too dry

to start over.

"Nothing is ruined, Nancy," Mom says.
"Every time I look at this, I'll think of
how much I love all of you!"
We sprinkle glitter on the cement.

JoJo thinks my footprints
look like a butterfly.
I guess you don't have to be perfect
to still be memorable!

Fancy Nancy's Fancy Words

These are the fancy words in this book:

Memorable—famous forever

Pizzazz—style

Devastated—disappointed